First American Edition 2017
Kane Miller, A Division of EDC Publishing

Text copyright © 2016 Chris Morphew, Rowan McAuley and David Harding
Illustration and design copyright © 2016 Hardie Grant Egmont
Illustration by Craig Phillips
Book cover design by Latifah Cornelius
First published in Australia by Hardie Grant Egmont 2016

For information contact:
Kane Miller, A Division of EDC Publishing
P.O. Box 470663
Tulsa, OK 74147-0663
www.kanemiller.com
www.edcpub.com
www.usbornebooksandmore.com

Library of Congress Control Number: 2016959848

Printed and bound in the United States of America
1 2 3 4 5 6 7 8 9 10

ISBN: 978-1-61067-660-1

THE
LOST HOME
WORLD

Cerberus Jones

Kane Miller
A DIVISION OF EDC PUBLISHING

CHAPTER ONE

"You're out, Floros!"

A cheer went up from most of the kids watching, and Erik grinned as Callan ran off to get the handball.

"No way!" Charlie stood still, refusing to budge, even though Shani had already stepped up to take his place.

"Come on, Charlie," said Callan, coming back with the ball and tossing it to Erik. "Don't be a sore loser."

"Yeah, Charlie," said Dean. "Just suck it up and let Shani have a turn."

1

"I've been waiting for ages, Charlie," said Shani, "and the bell's going to ring any minute now."

"But that ball was in," Charlie insisted.

Amelia, at the end of the line, looked up from her conversation with Sophie T. and winced. She hadn't been watching at the crucial moment, and had no idea what had happened.

"Seriously," Charlie said. "I can show you exactly where it bounced – right in the corner. It was the ultimate kill shot."

Erik crossed his arms. "It was out, Charlie. Stop whining about it and get lost, will you?"

"*Yeah*, Charlie." Callan was always quick to back Erik up.

Dean, being Shani's twin, was always going to take her side over Charlie's. And as for the rest, almost all the kids in Ms. Slaviero's class thought Charlie was a dork, and they were ready to let him know it.

Amelia watched Charlie's face redden into a stubborn, angry expression that was all too familiar for him at school. It didn't matter that he was probably right about that trick shot, the rest of the kids had decided he was done playing for the day.

Erik, seeing that he was about to lose his temper, pushed him one step further. "Oh, come on, Floros," he said in a falsely reasonable tone. "It's just a *game*. Just get out before you ruin it for everyone else, OK?"

Amelia heard an angry snort beside her, and suddenly Sophie T. was storming up to Erik. She flicked her long, blond hair back over one shoulder and pointed up at Erik. "*You* get out, Erik Zhang – that ball was in, and you know it."

Erik stared down at her in amazement, and a stunned silence fell over the whole school yard. Sophie T. was defending Charlie?

 3

"Uh, are you kidding me?" Erik asked her.

Charlie, as shocked as everyone else, nodded as though that was his question, too.

Amelia smiled. Last Saturday had been her birthday, and the first time Sophie T. had been over to her place – the old Gateway Hotel on the top of Forgotten Bay's headland. The party had started out well enough (loads of cake, fireworks, nice presents) but then a run-in with some intergalactic kidnappers had made a real mess of their night. With some help from Charlie, Sophie T. had avoided getting dragged through the gateway to another planet – but she'd found out all about the hotel's alien secrets.

She was sworn to silence by Gateway Control, of course. And so far, she'd done a brilliant job of keeping the secret to herself: since the night of the party, she had refused to even listen when Amelia and Charlie tried to discuss it with her.

"You're allowed to talk about it with *us*!" Amelia had promised, but Sophie T. wanted to pretend nothing had happened that weekend.

Right now, though, it was obvious that Sophie T. had changed. She'd never thought Charlie was just a goofy misfit like everyone else – the whole of Forgotten Bay knew she found him the most irritating, painful, disgusting, ridiculous and horrible boy on the planet. And Charlie felt exactly the same way about her. But now ...

"Do I look like I'm kidding, Erik?" Sophie T. put her hands on her hips. "You think you can boss Charlie around because everyone will back you up, but you're a cheater and a liar and worse than that: you're jealous because Charlie's better than you at handball."

Erik gaped at her.

And then Callan laughed, "Is that really you, Sophie T., or have you been abducted by aliens?"

5

All the kids laughed, but Sophie T. went white. Amelia ran to her side, a big fake smile on her face, and said, "Ha-ha, Callan, very funny. I *don't* think," and dragged Sophie T. away from the center of attention.

Forget all the dangers and secrets and crazy goings-on at the hotel – how long could Amelia and Charlie keep acting normal at school? How long before Forgotten Bay realized that none of this was a joke?

After school, Amelia and Charlie stopped off at Archie's grocery on the way home. The groundskeeper Tom had given them another one of his weird shopping lists: ten tubes of gel toothpaste and a large jar of whole grain mustard.

"It's got to be for Leaf Man," said Charlie as they began the steep walk up to the headland.

"Maybe," said Amelia. "It's been a week since we saw him, so he's due for another visit, isn't he?"

Leaf Man wasn't his real name, of course, but Amelia and Charlie didn't know what else to call the mysterious Keeper of the Gates and Ways, and he *did* like eating gum tree leaves. He was an alien, but totally unlike any other because instead of traveling through the wormholes that connected to the gateway, Leaf Man traveled through the Nowhere – the huge and dangerous space *between* the wormholes. And he seemed to know more about the gateway than anyone else – even more than Control did.

When Amelia and Charlie got past the hotel's gates, though, and trudged their way through the magnolias to Tom's cottage, there was no Leaf Man. Tom was tinkering with some holo-emitters at his desk, and stretched out on the sofa with a stack of charts was –

"James?" said Amelia, scowling at her older brother. His high school was in the city, more than an hour away by bus: no way should he be back yet. "What are you doing home from school again? Are you in trouble? Oh!" she gasped. "Did you get expelled again?"

"Expelled?" said Charlie, impressed. "What did you do?"

"I wasn't expelled," James sighed. "And I'm not in trouble now, either."

"Then what –"

"Are you my mum?" James interrupted her. "No. So let me and Tom get on with our work in peace."

Tom snorted and scratched under his eye patch. "Good luck."

"We're working, too," said Charlie, dumping the bags of toothpaste and mustard in Tom's kitchen.

"What are you working on?" Amelia asked James, by way of an apology.

James huffed, but he couldn't help himself – he was so excited by the gateway, he was always happy to talk about it. "I'm trying to work out how the gateway is controlled."

Tom straightened up at his desk, startled. "Controlled? Don't be ridiculous! You know how unpredictable and chaotic the wormholes are. There's nothing controlled there, believe me."

"Chaotic, yes," said James, "but not random. It can't be. I mean, look –"

He opened up a notebook and scrawled across a blank page:

$$0.00000000000000000004\%$$

"That's how much of the universe is matter, and not just empty space. Then imagine subtracting from that tiny number all the bits of matter that are comets, meteors, gas planets, dust clouds, stars, or planets without a breathable atmosphere. And then tell me: what are the chances that these wormholes are just *coincidentally* only connecting with a safe planet *every single time*?"

Amelia goggled at him, but Tom snorted. "Safe? Have you noticed what's been coming through the gateway lately?"

James shrugged. "The aliens aren't always nice, I admit, but the *wormholes* are safe. I mean, what's stopping one connecting us to a black hole? No, *something* must be organizing and directing the gateway system. If only we could work out what it was, or how it operated, then maybe we could understand why the wormholes are getting so off schedule."

James's eyes were shining with the possibilities, but Tom snapped, "Are you quite finished? Because unless I'm the only one who remembers what's been going on here, we've got more to worry about than theories and timetables. We've had a plague of cyborg rat spies, a time-shifter trying to rip the universe in half to get her hands on a canister more powerful than a nuclear bomb, and a continual stream of aliens trying to kidnap as many of us as they can." He drew in an angry breath while all three kids gazed at him. Amelia felt not only intimidated by his temper, but also vaguely guilty for being there when he lost it.

Tom blinked, as if suddenly realizing the effect he was having. He said in a milder voice, "Science is all very well in times of peace, James, but right now we have to stick to what's practical. For me, that means forgetting the hows and whys, and concentrating all our attention on what's going to come through the gateway next. And tell me, when's the last time it was anything good?"

At that moment the cottage was flooded with the most heavenly perfume, and a trill of ecstatic birdsong sounded from the stone stairwell in the next room. A new wormhole had connected.

CHAPTER TWO

James, still sitting with the charts, frowned and stared intently at the numbers. He looked at another chart for comparison. "This doesn't make any sense. Either this is that wormhole that never turned up a week ago, or the next wormhole on the schedule is nine hours early."

Tom snorted and got up from his desk. "The next wormhole is supposed to be from Klal Guinee, and that place stinks of volcanic ash. This is something else."

"What?" said Charlie.

"I don't know, but I'm getting my gun before we find out."

Amelia blanched. Tom had always been wary of the gateway, but meeting arrivals with a gun pointed at them was a whole new level.

Another gust of perfume blew up from the gateway stairs, stronger than before, and it seemed to Amelia to smell of nectar and strawberries and maybe the tiniest whiff of cinnamon. Amelia breathed it in deeply and felt very calm and yet hopeful, sure that something wonderful was about to happen, even with the sound of Tom loading his shotgun behind her. She turned to the gateway room and waited to see who or what would come up the stairs.

"Stand aside," said Tom, but both Amelia and Charlie ignored him, transfixed.

Perhaps it was the delight in the birdsong that held them because unlike any Earth bird Amelia had ever heard sing, this one didn't just sound beautiful. It was clearly and unarguably *happy*.

And then there was a soft rushing sound – like the hiss of water on the sand when the waves pull back from the shore – and the song was gone. The gateway had closed. But the perfume stayed as strong. In fact, Amelia was sure it was getting stronger. Almost too strong, too delicious to bear, but she and Charlie stayed where they were nonetheless, watching the edge of the stairwell in the next room.

Amelia heard a rustling of fabric, the gradually louder tapping of light shoes on the stone steps, and then at last their visitor emerged.

He was a young man – a human man, apparently – and something in his face made Amelia's heart pound. It wasn't just because he was beautiful, although he certainly was that. Not merely attractive or handsome or even gorgeous, he was *beautiful* in a way that made your eyes want to drink him up.

Amelia was almost befuddled by his beauty, but there was still more to it than that. What made Amelia really unsure of herself was how *familiar* he seemed. His hair was thick and black and held off his face with an intricate metal headband like a crown. He had smooth, tawny skin, sharp cheekbones and slanting gray eyes that were wide with excitement. He swept through the gateway room towards them so gracefully, his soft green robes just whispering over the floor, that Amelia almost curtsied.

"I see you've got your own holo-emitter," said Tom. "I'm afraid under Control's new orders, you'll have to exchange it for one of our registered units."

Amelia sighed. *Can't he keep this face for a while longer?*

But the alien put his hand up to his throat and firmly pressed his fingers to the spot where the holo-emitter should have been attached. "No holo-emitter here. This is just me."

James looked at his charts and jotted down some numbers in his notebook.

"You're human?" Charlie asked.

Amelia knew it wasn't always as simple as that. The Munfeep, for instance, were a shape-shifting species that could appear human with just a little borrowed DNA.

Nevertheless, Tom leaned his shotgun against the table and approached the alien to physically check for himself that there was no holo-emitter.

"No," said the man, smiling at Charlie so brilliantly that his eyes crinkled at the corners. His voice was warm and joyful. "Not human, though I could probably pass. I'm looking for the woman you call Lady Naomi."

Tom, his fingers just touching the alien's throat on both sides, suddenly reeled back, mouth open in shock. "Who are you?" He backed away, and reached behind him for his gun.

The man bowed his head. "My name is Mallan, and I am her brother."

Tom staggered back. His gun dropped to the floor, but he barely seemed to notice it fall.

Amelia finally tore her eyes away from the alien and glanced at Tom, puzzled. She'd never realized Lady Naomi had a brother either, but surely it wasn't that surprising ... was it?

Tom pulled himself together and said, rather roughly, "I suppose you have proof?"

"I have a memory," said Mallan, and from inside his robes, he took a flat box, about the size of a sandwich, and set it on the palm of his hand. With one finger, he prodded a wheel on the side, and a tiny crystal appeared in the center of the box. It flared with light and then suddenly they were looking at a baby lying on its back and playing with its feet.

"It's a holo-emitter!" said Charlie.

Mallan nodded. "Similar."

James looked more interested in the gadget than the image it was producing, but Tom had gone pale. "That's a baby," he said, gruff as ever. "They all look the same. This proves nothing."

"Wait."

Amelia looked at the baby and saw that it was moving – this wasn't a 3-D photo, but a 3-D video. And then she heard the baby gurgling to itself, and a woman's voice: she spoke in a rush of alien language, but the last word was clearly *Mallan*.

A boy about Amelia and Charlie's age ran into the image and scooped up the baby, plonking it in his lap and tickling its chubby belly until it broke into giggles. The boy grinned up at the camera, and Amelia could see it had to be Mallan: the same angular black eyebrows, the same wide smile. And then the woman came into the shot and cuddled up behind Mallan and the baby, beaming at the camera and speaking again. Mallan grabbed the baby's hand and made it wave while he repeated the woman's words.

Amelia had no idea what they were saying, but it hardly mattered. All four humans were staring at the mother of Mallan and the baby. She looked just like Lady Naomi.

No, not quite, Amelia corrected herself. Her nose was a little broader, and her hair was slightly purple rather than the true black of Lady Naomi and Mallan's, but it was proof all right.

Tom leaned heavily against the wall. "When was that taken?"

"Nearly twenty Earth years ago," Mallan said sadly. "She was not yet six months old."

Tom nodded thoughtfully, and then his head jerked up and he snapped, "And what was wrong with you people? Why did you let her near a gateway? What did you *think* would –"

He broke off, shaking his head. With a sudden rush of energy, he jumped up and grabbed Mallan by the arm, pulling him towards the door. "Right, come on, then – Mallan, was it? Let's find your sister."

Mallan staggered after him. His beautiful face broke into a smile so dazzling Amelia was dumbfounded. How could anything so angelic seem familiar to her?

"Come on," said Charlie, tugging on Amelia's elbow as he followed Mallan out the door.

It's because he's like Lady Naomi, of course. Amelia shook herself, and she and James hurried outside to catch up with the others.

Tom had already limped his way through the

magnolia grove, and together the five of them made their way up the hill, past the hedge maze, and towards the hidden bush track that led to Lady Naomi's workstation.

Charlie could hardly contain his impatience at Tom's stolid pace. "Tom, what's –" he asked. "How long have you and Lady Naomi known each other, anyway?"

Tom didn't answer. He crashed through the bush, one hand still locked around Mallan's arm. "Naomi! *Naomi!*"

Amelia and Charlie had time to exchange one last baffled glance before Lady Naomi slipped suddenly into view ahead of them, ducking gracefully under the low-hanging banksia branch that covered the beginning of her bush track. She looked startled to see a crowd of people headed in her direction, and then did a double take at the sight of Mallan.

She stood very still and waited until they were only a couple of feet away before she said quietly, "What's going on, Tom?"

Mallan stepped towards her, his face bright, but Lady Naomi fixed her eyes on Tom instead. "Who is this?"

Tom coughed, then laid his hand on Lady Naomi's arm and said very gently, "It's your brother."

Lady Naomi stiffened, her eyes wide with shock, and yet so like Mallan's.

Amelia didn't know what she'd expected – perhaps whoops of excitement, or maybe weeping and laughter like the Munfeep, or just a thousand questions – but instead Lady Naomi stayed right where she was, utterly still, and only stared and stared as Mallan drew closer. He stopped in front of her. The two of them stood gazing silently at each other, and Amelia's mouth fell open as it suddenly dawned on her that they were meeting for the first time – or at least, for the *first time* since Lady Naomi was old enough to remember.

The air between them was electric, and Amelia couldn't believe anything so quiet and motionless could feel so explosive.

The two extraordinary faces studied each other, and Amelia saw they had the same hairline, the same foreheads, and though Mallan was slightly taller than Lady Naomi and dressed like a prince, while she was in her usual cargo pants, they wore exactly the same expressions. And at almost exactly the same moment, tears spilled down exactly the same angular cheekbones.

Lady Naomi slowly reached out her hand, and whispered, "Are you really here?"

Mallan reached out and set his palm against hers, perfectly symmetrical, and whispered back, "You must have so many questions. We've got plenty for you too. That's why I'm here. We've been looking for you for a long time, Oriana. I've come to bring you home."

CHAPTER THREE

"*Oriana*," Tom muttered. "All along ... Oriana ..."

He was sitting at the table in the lounge, staring into a mug of black tea. Mum and Mary swapped worried looks, and Dad dumped another heaped spoon of sugar into Tom's mug.

Mum had given Mallan one of the guest rooms to stay in, and he and Lady Naomi were up there right now. His holo-projector was filled with dozens of other clips of Lady Naomi's long-lost family, and obviously Lady Naomi was desperate to see them all.

More than that, Amelia could tell that Lady

Naomi – or were they supposed to call her Oriana now? – was self-conscious about crying in front of them before. She was an extremely private person, and so no way did she want to discover her whole family background with everyone watching.

Still, it felt weird to be down here together – *all the humans*, Amelia supposed – with Lady Naomi upstairs with some alien brother who'd appeared out of nowhere. Weird that this stranger could have already put such a huge distance between them and Lady Naomi. Mum always said, "Blood's thicker than water," and Amelia had never liked the idea. Sure, family was important, but how quickly would Lady Naomi forget all her friends?

James was still scowling over the charts, trying to figure out where Mallan's wormhole had come from. "None of these figures add up," he said for about the hundredth time. "Tom, you must know something about the wormhole Lady Naomi arrived through."

Tom shook his head, refusing to look up, and seemed unable to speak.

"Tom?" said Dad gently. "What can you tell us?"

Tom heaved a deep sigh and then said, "Almost nothing."

Charlie, who had been heroically quiet up until now, blurted out, "Weren't you there?"

"I was."

They all waited. Amelia was torn between desperately wanting to know everything, and not wanting to see Tom get any more upset.

At last he said, "I'm not going to go into all the details. I explained it all once, back then, and I expect Control would show you the report I made, if you must see it. I don't ever want to talk about it again, but ..." His mouth twisted.

"It's enough to say that this happened at the height of the Guild war – the *end* of it, as it turned out, though we didn't know it then."

"The Guild again!" spluttered Charlie. "Who are those guys? I always just imagine Control, but with black capes and helmets."

"The Guild are nothing like Control." Tom's face was curiously blank, as though his attention were turned so far inside, the words were coming almost without his knowledge. "Gateway Control was cobbled together from what was left of the resistance when the war ended, to make sure the Guild never came back."

Amelia and Charlie glanced at each other. They'd always thought of Control as this vast, all-powerful authority, but really it hadn't even been around as long as the Forgotten Bay Surf Club.

"But the Guild," Tom went on, "are ancient – older than half the civilizations they've conquered and destroyed. Before the gateway evolved, they were just ordinary merchants: generations of families living on cargo cruisers the size of planetoids, drifting from star system to star system over centuries to trade their goods.

"And then they discovered the gateways, and realized that journeys that took several lifetimes by ship could be made in mere moments by wormhole. And trade that had only ever been in metals, stone and other ageless materials could be replaced by far more lucrative things. At first, they made fortunes in fabrics, perfumes and spices, then almost overnight, they moved on to weapons, drugs and slaves."

Tom closed his eye, his voice toneless. "Thousands of years of secretive and fiercely loyal family networking was converted more or less instantly into a criminal organization that held whole galaxies for ransom."

Amelia gulped. She was finally beginning to understand just how big the war must have been, and how much had been at stake. Control's strict rules about who could use the gateways, and how, suddenly didn't seem ridiculous at all.

Tom opened his eye and stared blankly at Charlie. "Eventually, gateway by gateway, the resistance managed to build. And once that happened, war over the gateway system was inevitable."

He shook himself. "Anyway, there are history files on all of this. It's enough to say that twenty years ago, it was chaos around the gateway. The wormholes were more unpredictable and violent than at any time in their history, until ... well, *now*. And Guild and Resistance fighters were streaming through, coming and going with every connection, constantly fleeing one battlefield and charging into the next. Some wormholes arrived with nothing but the dead and injured to deliver

– they were fighting even as they traveled. Some were sucked into the Nowhere, so desperate to escape whatever was chasing them they didn't wait for the wormholes to align."

"And this was all happening in your cottage?" said Charlie.

"Some of it. More went on down in the caves below us. Some of it spilled up into the hotel. In fact, the Resistance set up a camp hospital in the library. But anyway ... Sometime in the middle of the night, when things had been unexpectedly quiet for a couple of hours, I went back to my cottage, hoping to save some of the tech and charts I'd been forced to abandon earlier. And I heard crying from the bottom of the gateway stairs."

"Lady Naomi?" said Amelia.

Tom almost smiled. "That's what we called her. Naomi – my little lady. She was just a baby – too young to speak or even crawl, just lying on her back, naked and alone. It still gives me nightmares to imagine what would have happened to her if I hadn't found her."

"She arrived just as you did?" asked James. "About what time was that? And do you remember the day? I'm sure if I tried hard enough I could figure ..."

Tom held up a hand. "It's no good. We tried, but no one can be really sure how long Lady Naomi had been lying there before I heard her. She had the beginnings of hypothermia, so it could have been nearly half a day. And, as I said before, the wormholes had been wild – blowbacks, misconnections, and entirely unscheduled arrivals all over the place."

"You mean, Lady Naomi has been here almost her whole life?" said Dad.

"Oh, Tom," said Mum. "You raised her yourself?"

"Not exactly. Not at first, anyway. It was

Caroline who became Lady Naomi's mother – the old housekeeper," he explained. "I was more like a ... er, an uncle or something."

Amelia suspected he had been a bit more involved than that, but nobody wanted to push him any further right now. Then she wondered all over again about Lady Naomi herself. *Imagine knowing you were an alien, that Earth wasn't really your home – and yet never having the first clue about where you'd come from.*

It was tough enough for Charlie not knowing where his dad was, and he at least had a mum and a country and the rest of the human race.

The first time Krskn had seen Lady Naomi, even he – the big-shot alien mercenary who thought he knew everything – had been baffled by her. Amelia could still hear the icy curiosity in his voice as he took her in for the first time.

"And you ... What might you be, my dear?"

It had sounded creepy at the time, but now Amelia realized it must have also been a painful question for Lady Naomi. And what about Caroline? What had happened to her? Why had she been Lady Naomi's mother only "at first"? Had Lady Naomi lost her family *twice*?

But Charlie's mind had followed a different train of thought. "So *that's* what her research is about!" he said suddenly. "Right? She's been looking for her home."

Tom nodded.

"But if she wanted to go looking for her family ... why stay here on Earth? Why not actually *go looking*? Head out through the gateway, and –"

"Why not –" Tom choked, growing suddenly angry. "Why not just run blindfolded out onto the highway? Why not just go skydiving without a parachute? What do I keep telling you people? The gateway is *dangerous*! Have you never wondered where Lady Naomi got that *scar* on her arm?"

Amelia gulped. All along, Tom had been yelling at them about the dangers of the gateway, and even though she'd listened, and basically knew he was right, she'd always thought he was exaggerating a bit, the way adults usually do.

For her and Charlie, the gateway was a magic trick that kept bringing them adventure. For Dad and James, it was pure science and an endless set of mathematical puzzles. But for Tom, it was a battlefield that ate up soldiers and spat out the dying, and once, by accident, a baby girl he loved. And then the thing that sliced up her arm so badly she had a silvery snake of scar tissue from wrist to shoulder to this day.

No wonder he was touchy about it. And no wonder he was protective of Lady Naomi. What would it mean for Tom if Lady Naomi accepted Mallan's offer to take her home?

CHAPTER FOUR

The next day at school took forever to finish. Charlie always squirmed in class, but even Amelia found it impossible to concentrate on what Ms. Slaviero was saying when every second away from the hotel was another second of lost time with Lady Naomi. Surely she and Charlie could catch up on their schoolwork *after* Lady Naomi had left the face of Earth. It was OK for James – whatever was going on with him, their parents had agreed to let him take the whole day off school.

It's so unfair, thought Amelia. *What if Lady*

Naomi is gone by the time we get home and I never get to say good-bye?

"Earth to Amelia Walker," said Ms. Slaviero. "Come in, Commander Walker – report your status, please."

Amelia blinked as she realized the whole class was looking at her. "Um ... present, miss."

"Are you sure?" Ms. Slaviero smiled. "Because from here, you looked like you were out on a space walk."

"Sorry, Ms. Slaviero."

"No, no." She waved away the apology. "I've collected some valuable negative information here: you've helped me see we've spent enough time on photosynthesis for now. Let's take a five-minute disco break. OK, class – you've got forty-five seconds to push back the tables and clear the dance floor while I put the music on."

"Nice work." Sophie T. grinned at Amelia,

putting her pencils and books away. "What *were* you thinking about, anyway? You looked really worried."

Amelia leaned over and whispered, "Lady Naomi's brother arrived yesterday."

Sophie T.'s eyes grew round. "She has a brother? What's he like?"

"He's just like Lady Naomi."

"Amazing, you mean?"

"Yeah, but ..." Amelia frowned.

Ms. Slaviero's stereo began to blast out "I Will Survive" and Amelia felt more frustrated than ever. She shoved her desk back with more force than necessary, not able to explain even to herself why she was so ... What was it? It was more than worry about how much she was going to miss Lady Naomi.

Maybe she was just being a totally selfish little baby, acting as if she'd rather Lady Naomi had never been found by her family, but she couldn't shake a gnawing sense of resentment.

When at last the bell rang, Amelia and Charlie raced back to the headland. But where to look first? Tom's? The hotel? Perhaps they were already too late.

"Relax," said Mary, watching them from the hotel's verandah as they thundered up the driveway. "Lady Naomi's taken Mallan down to her workstation. James is with them, so it'll probably be OK if you go, too."

"Thanks, Mary," said Amelia.

"Bye, Mum," said Charlie, and without another word, they dumped their bags on the top step and ran down the hill again, this time towards Lady Naomi's hidden bush track.

"I suppose putting these away is my job, is it?"

Mary called after them, but they were long gone.

Crashing along the narrow path, around the last corner, and into Lady Naomi's clearing, they saw that her workstation was up and running, with Mallan leaning over the controls. Lady Naomi stood close beside him.

James was practically vibrating with jealousy, and Amelia could understand why. He'd been itching to get his hands on this alien technology for ages, but Lady Naomi had never let anyone else touch it. Not even Control, when they'd used the site to hide a starship.

Lady Naomi had no hesitation about sharing her stuff with Mallan, though. She beamed with joy, and gave him free rein to play with all the settings. As Amelia and Charlie approached, they could smell that the whole clearing was filled with that perfume that hung around Mallan.

"Look," he was saying to his sister. "This is our

galaxy – it's on the far side of this super cluster. I don't know if Earth has identified it yet, but we call it the Great Oriana."

Lady Naomi looked surprised and, if possible, even more delighted.

"Yes," Mallan laughed. "Mum and Dad named you after the galaxy. I was named after some distant uncle, so I think we all know who was the favorite." He grinned at her with that incredible smile that was so strangely familiar to Amelia, and then turned back to the equipment.

"Let me zoom in – ah, here is our solar system, with our sun, Karaskon at the center, and *here* –" he focused in on a dot circling the star "– is our planet, Chloros. Well," he frowned slightly at the blurry smudge on the screen, "that's not a great visual, but try to imagine a planet that is almost entirely green. We don't have oceans like Earth, but thousands of rivers crisscrossing the most fertile, lush forest and grassland you can imagine. And *there*, right near the equator, but high in the mountains where it's forever spring, is where our family lives. If you come home with me on the next gateway connection, we will be back in time for you to see the great migration of the succubees – iridescent butterflies the size of Earth's pelicans, each one the color of the flower it last fed on."

James, peering at the figures listed at the bottom of the screen, scribbled in his notebook.

Amelia felt herself growing dizzy at the beauty of the world Mallan was describing. How much more wonderful it must be for Lady Naomi, knowing that not only was she going to go there – she *belonged* there. It would be awful for the rest of them when Lady Naomi left, but how could anyone ask her to stay?

"But our parents," Lady Naomi said, almost reluctantly, as though she didn't want to bring up anything that would break the spell of Mallan's words. "They're both gone?"

Mallan's lovely face became grave, and he laid a hand on her arm. Amelia noticed James wince, and realized she was clenching her jaw. Lady Naomi had always been friendly, but somehow untouchable. Not aloof, but sort of separate, like royalty. It felt strange and even presumptuous to Amelia to see him handling Lady Naomi so casually.

"Yes. I'm sorry you never got to know them." Then he smiled. "But our grandmother is still alive, and from the day I told her I'd finally tracked you down, she's been calling in cousins and aunts and uncles and all our friends and clan members. By the time we get back, half the mountain people of Chloros will be lined up to welcome you. Not least," he ducked his head shyly, "my wife and our three children."

"I'm an aunt?" Lady Naomi gasped, and Amelia knew the deal was done. The wonder of a home planet was powerful, but the promise of blood relatives who already loved her was beyond anything Earth could offer. Poor Tom was no competition.

"*Grawk!*"

They heard the sharp bark before they saw him. Amelia turned, already smiling at the arrival of her friend, but then stopped, shocked by Grawk's appearance. Since his growth spurt, he'd been hiding out more and more in the bush, avoiding almost everyone but Amelia. She missed hanging out with him as much as she used to, but was glad he was being so careful around strangers.

Now, though, he came springing through the trees, his blunt ears laid back against his head, and all fear of exposure apparently forgotten. His teeth were bared, and his eyes narrowed to slits. He landed silently in the clearing, not even snapping a twig as his enormous paws hit the ground, and stared at Mallan.

Mallan paled, and who could blame him? Grawk wasn't growling, but every now and then he lashed his tail.

Amelia looked at Charlie in alarm. Grawk had never made a mistake yet about who was friend and who was foe. So if Grawk didn't like Mallan ...

But Lady Naomi wasn't fazed. "Grawk!" she scolded him. "Stop messing around. That's my brother you're bullying. Be nice, will you?"

She laid a hand protectively on Mallan's arm, and Grawk glanced at her. "See?" she went on. "There's no problem."

Grawk stopped flicking his tail, and reluctantly eased off his snarl until all those razor-sharp teeth were neatly hidden. His ears, though, stayed flat to his skull, and he kept a steady gaze on Mallan.

"Is that –" Mallan began, then gulped. "What is that?"

"This is Grawk," said Lady Naomi. "Grawk, this is Mallan."

Mallan's eyes widened, and Amelia could guess why. Even if you'd never heard of grawks before, Grawk would be frightening. But if you had, then you'd know they were one of the universe's most ferocious and intelligent beasts. You'd also know they didn't grow much bigger than a wombat, and yet here was Grawk, as big as a tiger and twice as broad.

And probably hungry, too, Amelia thought. She had no idea what he'd been eating out here in the bush, but she doubted it was gum tree leaves. Maybe he'd been attracted by Mallan's delicious fragrance.

Maybe, because as Lady Naomi smiled at him and said to Mallan, "Go on, hold out your hand

and let him smell you," Grawk licked his lips with a huge purple tongue.

Mallan flinched, but he did as his sister asked and walked three or four cautious steps towards Grawk. She came with him, murmuring encouragement.

"Here, boy," he said doubtfully, holding out a hand that trembled slightly. Behind him, James grimaced in sympathy.

Grawk flicked his tail once more, but stretched out to sniff Mallan's knuckles. Amelia held her breath. Whether or not Mallan knew it, this would be a bigger proof of his identity than even a million holo-videos of family. They just proved that he was Lady Naomi's brother; Grawk would decide whether he was a good one.

Grawk sniffed, blinked, and crept forward another half pace. Mallan stiffened, but Lady Naomi stood calmly beside him, and he stayed where he was.

Grawk sniffed again, and then sneezed violently. He looked so shocked at himself, Amelia almost laughed. He sniffed once more, his ears pricked forward now and his tail slightly wagging, though his eyes were confused. He whined, then leapt back and started sneezing helplessly.

"Oh, Grawk, you poor thing," Lady Naomi said. "Look at what you've done, Mallan – you've given him hay fever."

Mallan laughed with her. "Sorry, buddy," he said to Grawk. "I didn't mean to, well, get up your nose like that. No hard feelings, eh?"

Grawk, wracked by sneezes, could only wag his tail feebly, his ears back. Amelia considered what that meant. She didn't think that Grawk liked Mallan, but he seemed to have accepted him.

Maybe that was all that any of them had to do. After all, it would be hard to really like anyone

who took Lady Naomi away from them, but as long as Lady Naomi was happy, what did it matter? Knowing that all her years of research had ended with the greatest possible discovery, knowing that she would be reunited with her family at last – well, that would have to be enough for them.

CHAPTER FIVE

Sophie T. was no huge fan of Grawk's and had no interest in discussing his odd behavior with Amelia at school the next day. She wanted to hear only about Mallan. "I wish I could meet him," she sighed. "He sounds gorgeous."

Amelia grimaced and looked to Charlie for help.

"You could come up to the hotel with us," said Charlie, which was not only the polite thing to say, but also the best way to get Sophie T. to drop the subject. She'd made it pretty clear that she never wanted to go near the headland or its gateway ever again.

When they got home that afternoon, Amelia realized there was no time for Sophie T. to visit anyway. Going into Tom's cottage to drop off some anchovy spread and laundry soap, they found that Lady Naomi's farewell had already begun.

"So you're going tomorrow, then?" Tom was saying, concentrating on the holo-emitter he was working on.

"Mallan thinks so," said Lady Naomi. "Obviously the wormholes are unreliable at the moment, but yes ... by nightfall tomorrow, he says."

James spun the cogs on his new gadget for calculating wormhole arrivals, and frowned down at his charts. Amelia saw him write in his notebook, pull out more charts, and frown again.

"I'd like us to spend the day here, if we can," Mallan smiled at Tom, but all his blinding handsomeness just bounced off the top of Tom's head. "Naturally, Oriana wants to be with you as much as possible before we leave, and I don't want to risk missing the connection."

Tom grunted, then looked up at Lady Naomi. "I'll sort out your registration with Control. They usually like a couple of weeks to process identity documents and run background checks, but I know Ms. Rosby will help us rush it through."

It was hardly the most sentimental speech, but Amelia knew how much Tom meant by it. Although it was breaking his heart, he would help Lady Naomi to leave.

Mallan must have understood that too because he caught Amelia's eye and nodded towards the door. She nodded back: he was right – she and Charlie should get out of there for a while and give Tom some time alone with Lady Naomi.

She tugged on Charlie's elbow. They tiptoed towards the door, trying to avoid attention. James, taking the hint, bundled up his charts and followed them out. Amelia was surprised to find that Mallan had come too.

"I don't think Tom needs me around right now," he smiled sadly. "I should have realized it before I came – of course Oriana would have a whole life here on Earth."

"Not much of a life," said Charlie. "All she ever does is her research out in the bush. She never leaves the headland at all, not even to surf."

"Ah, but she has people who care for her – who'll miss her," Mallan countered. "People who, even though they're glad she's found her answers, must be distressed that one of those answers will take her away."

"We're not really angry at you," Amelia blurted

55

out. Then she realized she'd basically admitted he was right: she resented him. She blushed.

Mallan gave her one of his most blazing smiles, one that made her tingle all the way through as though she'd been given an electric shock, and said, "You can't imagine how happy I am to know that Oriana is so loved."

He put a hand over his face, as though overcome with emotion, then blinked away any lingering tears and gave another, rather wobbly, smile. "We were so frightened."

"Eh?" said Charlie. "Of what? Us?"

"No – we were frightened that you didn't exist. We always hoped Oriana had landed somewhere safe, but we could never quite believe she had. For all we knew, that helpless baby landed in a war zone –"

"She did," said Charlie, but Mallan went on.

"Or a desert, or in the middle of an ocean. And

sometimes, we almost wished she had because what if something even worse had happened to her instead? What if people did find her and keep her alive, but not to be kind – what if they were cruel, or kept her as a slave?"

"That's awful!" said Amelia.

Out of the corner of her eye, she saw James open his mouth to say something, but Mallan said, "But it wasn't awful! It so easily could have been, but look at this place!" He beamed at the landscape. "It's dry and hot compared to Chloros, but so beautiful. And perhaps it has been a lonelier life for Oriana than it would have been in our mountains, but she has had a family here. I can't tell you how glad that makes me.

"Anyway," he went on cheerfully. "It's not like I'm taking her away forever, is it? The wormholes to Chloros aren't super-frequent, but Oriana will definitely be coming and going between her homes."

"About that," said James, holding up a chart. "I still can't figure out which wormhole connects to Chloros. We don't seem to have any record of it here."

Amelia and Charlie stared at James, but Mallan was unruffled. "Of course not. We're on a completely different hub. To get to Chloros, we have to travel to one of the three planets with the two gateways we need: one that connects to the Earth hub, and one that connects to the Janys hub. It's like ... it's like ..." He searched for a comparison.

"No, I get it," said James, still frowning. "You're basically just changing trains halfway."

"Exactly!" Mallan grinned.

"OK," said James. "That makes sense, I guess."

"Well, it makes travel more complicated, certainly."

"But will we see you again?" Amelia pressed.

"You and Lady Naomi? You definitely will come back?"

"Better than that," Mallan said. "I've heard rumors that things are starting to change at Control. If that's right, the whole non-stellar planet category could be scrapped."

"You mean –"

"Yes. Earth could be allowed to know about the gateway and you could start using it yourselves."

Amelia and Charlie hardly dared believe their ears.

Mallan leaned down, his wonderful gray eyes becoming even more angular as he grinned. "Perhaps you won't have to say good-bye to Oriana when we visit next. Perhaps instead you will be able to come back with us and see Chloros for yourselves."

Amelia stared, too overwhelmed to speak. All her reserve about Mallan, all her dread of Lady

Naomi going, and all her jealousy that Mallan had straightaway been more special to Lady Naomi than Amelia would ever be – all of it suddenly seemed not just petty or mean, but irrelevant. She was being invited to Chloros!

She breathed in his sweet smell, and was entranced by the vision his words built in her mind. She imagined herself, ordinary old Amelia Walker, being led out by Mallan and Lady Naomi into a green world where butterflies soared through the sky like eagles.

Maybe we're not losing Lady Naomi after all, she marveled. *Maybe we're all getting to be part of something bigger instead. Something better than any of us imagined.*

She remembered that hopefulness she'd felt when Mallan first stepped through the gateway, and sighed.

It really is going to be all right.

CHAPTER SIX

Amelia and Charlie didn't even try to sleep that night. Mary had agreed to let Charlie stay over so he could say good-bye to Lady Naomi in the morning before school, just in case she and Mallan left before they got home again in the afternoon.

Charlie was on the old single bed in Amelia's room, and Amelia was sprawled on her huge four-poster, but neither of them had bothered to change into their pajamas, let alone get into bed. They were both too worried that Lady Naomi and Mallan's plans might suddenly change, and they wanted to be ready to spring up without delay. Plus, there was so much to talk about –

Like whether everyone on Chloros was as stunning and charismatic as Lady Naomi and Mallan, or whether they were as freakishly perfect at home as they were on Earth. And whether the gravity would be different there. And what the food would be like. And whether *they'd* have to wear holo-emitters to fit in and understand the language, or whether Lady Naomi would be patient enough to help them learn it for themselves. And, most importantly to Charlie, whether you could train one of their giant butterflies to carry you in its legs like a living hang glider.

They were just getting started on whether or not they could take Grawk with them when they heard footsteps pounding along the corridor outside Amelia's bedroom, and then someone thumping on Mum and Dad's door.

Leaping off their beds, Charlie flung open the door, and they saw James getting ready to knock again. He looked utterly frantic.

Mum opened the door. "What? What is it? No – don't tell me out here, come in. And *be quiet,* will you? We do have six rooms booked in the guest wing."

She ushered James inside, then caught sight of Amelia and Charlie – so prepared for action, they were actually wearing shoes – and sighed. "You too. Might as well let you in on it from the start, eh?"

Grinning to themselves, Amelia and Charlie scampered into Mum and Dad's room. Dad was still in bed, wearing a faded old *Kiss the Cook* T-shirt, but no glasses.

"What's the emergency?" he asked, feeling around on his bedside table for glasses.

"There's no Chloros!" James said. "I've checked and rechecked all the charts, all the records, even all the Control catalogs of all known stellar planets – *there is no Chloros!*"

Mum frowned. "But it's just a name, James. I mean, we say Germany, but Germans say *Deutschland*. We say China, but Chinese say *Zhongguo*. Control could easily call Chloros something else."

"No! It's more than that!" James was trying so hard not to shout, but his eyes were wild. "I can't find any mention of Karaskon, their system's sun, *or –*" he rushed on before Mum could make the same argument "– of any galaxy called the Great Oriana."

"Hmm," said Mum.

"And it's not just about the names. I checked out the coordinates of the planet Mallan showed us." James waved his notebook at them. "It doesn't have a gateway. In fact, in the planetary catalogs I found in Tom's storeroom, that planet is in what Control calls a *dead galaxy*."

Dad jerked in surprise. "A galaxy without a single gateway!"

James nodded, looking relieved that Dad at least was following him.

"But James, are you sure?" Mum asked. "I mean, some of those charts and books of Tom's are ancient – much older than Control. What if they use a different system of coordinates? Maybe you missed something. Like not understanding something is written in Fahrenheit instead of Celsius."

"Right," James agreed. "Which is why I called Control."

Mum spluttered, then realized there were bigger issues here than James going over his parents' heads and getting mixed up with Control.

"And?" said Dad, bracing himself.

"The coordinates are right. Mallan's so-called home world is a dead planet in a dead galaxy."

Mum looked at Dad for confirmation that James had really proven his argument. "Scott?"

"Mum! Call Control yourself if you don't believe me," snapped James.

"I believe you, James," said Dad. "But I still don't understand why Tom or Lady Naomi haven't picked up on this for themselves."

James waved his hands in exasperation. "*Why?* Have you seen them, Dad? Tom's practically gone zombie over Lady Naomi leaving, and Lady Naomi is so happy, I doubt she's thinking about anything except meeting her granny."

"Fair point. So you haven't told Tom?"

"I don't even know where he is! I was down in the cottage for hours working on this before I called Control. I was hoping he'd come back so I wouldn't have to, but he still hasn't."

Mum groaned. "He won't. He came up just before dinnertime and told me Control HQ needed him to come down to sort out Lady Naomi's paperwork in person before they could clear her to leave."

"But that doesn't make any sense, Skye!" said Dad. "If they needed anyone to see them *in person* it would have been Lady Naomi, not Tom."

"And in the middle of the night?" Amelia put in.

"All right!" Mum retorted. "But I didn't *believe* him. I thought he was just making an excuse to get out of town for a while. But now –"

"Yes?" said James.

"Now it seems more likely someone wanted Tom away from the gateway."

"Mallan," said Charlie.

"Right," said James.

"OK, OK, let's think." Mum closed her eyes.

"Is Mallan really Lady Naomi's brother? Irrelevant. Better question: are his intentions good? The evidence suggests not. He's told lies about where he comes from and where he plans to take Lady Naomi, so although it's *possible* he has a decent motive for hiding the truth from us, we need to assume –"

"That he's another creepy alien enemy," said Charlie.

"Exactly." Mum's eyes opened. "So, we organize. Scott, Mallan wanted Tom away from the gateway; you need to get down there now and guard it."

"Done." Dad slid out of bed, pulled sweatpants on over his pajama bottoms and grabbed his boots.

"You know Tom has a shotgun behind the front door?" Charlie said helpfully.

Amelia recoiled, but didn't protest. The only thing worse than the thought of her goofy, gentle dad with a gun was the thought of him totally alone and unarmed in Tom's cottage.

"It'll be fine, cookie," he said, kissing the top of her head as he walked out of the room.

"Next, James," said Mum. "We need to work out which wormhole Mallan is planning on catching tomorrow: what time, what planet, and from that – hopefully – we can tell what this is about."

James shook his head. "I'll try, but the charts have been so useless lately. I've checked over and over and I still can't tell where Mallan came *from*."

"Keep trying. But not at Tom's."

James was about to argue, but Mum spoke over him. "I'm sorry, James, but it's bad enough having Dad down there. I know there are more charts down there –"

"And my calculating cogs!"

"And those," Mum agreed, "but until we know what's going on, I need you as safe as can be. Even if that's not much safer."

"What about us?" said Amelia.

"You?" Mum blinked. "Why, you stay in your room with the door closed, of course. Hide under the bed, if you need to."

"But –"

Mum held up a hand. "No debating. We don't have time. Just wait here with James until I check on Lady Naomi."

Oh, yeah, Amelia thought. *We have to tell her what's going on.*

Mum slipped out to the hallway, and was back all too quickly. "She's gone. No one in her room, and no one in Mallan's. This escalates things. We need to assume the worst and work backward from there, and the worst-case scenario I can see is that Mallan has kidnapped Lady Naomi."

She bit her lip and thought hard. "OK, James – we last saw Lady Naomi at dinner. Widen your search to include any wormholes that have left since then. We may be too late to stop Mallan taking Lady Naomi, but if we can tell Control where he took her –"

"On it," said James, but he was pale.

"Now." Mum turned to Amelia and Charlie. "I know you hate this, but I also know you care too much about Lady Naomi to waste any time delaying me with arguments. I'm trusting you to go to your room, Amelia, and stay there until someone comes to tell you it's safe. OK?"

Amelia's heart pounded with frustration. She knew they could help, and wouldn't that make rescuing Lady Naomi quicker?

"Amelia?"

She shook her head, unable to answer, but to her shock, Charlie spoke for them both. "You can trust us, Mrs. Walker. We know the right thing to do."

CHAPTER SEVEN

Amelia stuffed her hands into her pockets so no one could see how tightly she was clenching her fists as Mum led her and Charlie back to her room.

"We'll let you know what's happening as soon as we can," Mum said apologetically.

"Don't worry, Mrs. Walker," said Charlie. "As long as Lady Naomi is OK, that's the main thing."

Amelia ground her teeth, and Mum closed the door, shutting them in.

Charlie heaved a great sigh. "She's gone."

"Yeah, I know she's gone!" Amelia snapped. "Which is why we should be out there helping her, not stuck in here like a couple of babies."

"Not Lady Naomi, you dope – your mum. I was afraid she was going to stay in and keep an eye on us all night."

"Why would she?" Amelia retorted. "You just promised her we'd stay right here."

"No, I didn't. I told her she could trust us to do the right thing."

"You –" Amelia looked hard at him. "You what?"

Charlie nodded. "Your mum was right about one thing: we don't have time to argue if we want to help Lady Naomi. That's why I didn't bother trying to convince them they're wrong about the whole wormhole thing."

"They are?"

"I'm pretty sure. I mean, at some stage, Mallan

will have to get a wormhole out of here, and maybe he'll even try to take Lady Naomi with him, but I don't think that's his number-one plan."

"Then what –" Amelia answered her own question: "Lady Naomi's workstation."

She started for her bedroom door, Charlie beside her.

"I bet," he whispered as they padded down the corridor. "I mean, think about it: he hardly needed to kidnap Lady Naomi, did he? She was ready to go willingly at any moment. And he didn't need to get rid of Tom because Tom said he'd help them go. So why would he vanish with her in the middle of the night? Unless he just loves the drama, I think he's after something else."

"But," Amelia whispered back, following his logic now, "Lady Naomi must still be necessary for Mallan to get what he wants, or why else go to all this trouble to con her?"

"Exactly."

"So you're right: he must want her equipment for something – and he needs her eyes and her fingerprints to scan in."

"Yeah." Charlie made a face. "So let's get down there before he decides what to do with the rest of her."

To avoid bumping into Mum, Amelia and Charlie slunk down the servants' stairs at the back of the hotel. They came out a narrow door near the ballroom deck, crossed the lawn to the edge of the hedge and paused. Luckily for them, it was a clear night – not the perfect brightness of the full moon they'd had on Amelia's disastrous birthday night, but enough of a fat gibbous moon to bathe the headland in silvery light.

Amelia could see right across the hillside.

There was no one to see, but anyone watching would easily see *them* as they cut across the grounds to Lady Naomi's track.

"We'll have to be quick," said Charlie, thinking along the same lines. "But we're both in dark clothes. I'm sure we'll be fine."

"Doesn't matter," said Amelia grimly. "It's got to be done, whether anyone sees us or not. I was just ... well, I wish Grawk were with us. Or at least, I wish I knew where he was."

"What would he do? Sneeze on Mallan?"

Amelia snorted, and they both crept out into the moonlight, leaving the safety of the hotel behind. Instinctively, they stayed as close to the edges of the grounds as possible, avoiding the direct route across the open grass. They managed to stay more or less in the shadows until they were most of the way down the hill.

Amelia scanned the hotel grounds once more,

but saw no sign of movement anywhere.

"All right," she whispered to Charlie. "Let's go."

They sprinted the last few feet to Lady Naomi's banksia tree, then slipped under its leaning trunk, and were in the bush. Somehow, being surrounded by all the trees felt safer, but only for a second. Almost as soon as Amelia had breathed a sigh of relief, she realized that not only did the bush hide them from Mallan, it would also hide Mallan from them. And though they would be harder to see, they would be much easier to *hear*, with all the dry leaves and twigs that snapped underfoot, and the spiny branches that rustled and cracked as they pushed through.

Both kids slowed their steps, slowed even their breathing, and trod as carefully as they could. Amelia watched out for the faint yellow glow of Grawk's eyes as much as for the shape of Mallan.

Then, just before the last turn in the path,

Amelia saw a huge heap of something blocking their way. She and Charlie stopped and stared, willing their eyes to see more clearly in the vague moonlight. A low grinding noise rumbled out of the mound, very faint, but unmistakable.

Amelia rushed forward and knelt in front of the heap. She reached out and ran her hands over the dense, velvety fur until she found the face that was so dear to her.

"Grawk?" she whispered, stroking his muzzle. "What has he done to you?"

He rumbled again, and one eye opened the merest slit. Amelia saw that his pupil was unnaturally narrow, and then the lid slumped closed again. He whined, but so faintly it might as well have been a sob.

"What's wrong with him?"

"Hang on." Charlie rummaged through his pockets and pulled out a tiny flashlight – an almost useless thing designed to hang off a key ring, but it gave just enough light for them to find the little dart in Grawk's shoulder. Amelia pulled it out. It was too late for that to help Grawk, but she hated seeing it there. She wrapped it in a dirty tissue she found in her jeans pocket and then put it under a rock. She'd find it later and show Dad and Control. Hopefully.

"Come on," said Charlie quietly, putting away his flashlight. "We can't help him, and we still haven't helped Lady Naomi."

"Sorry," Amelia said, kissing the soft fur of Grawk's head, then got up to follow Charlie.

They went achingly slowly now, knowing that with every step they took, it was easier for Mallan to hear them coming. And they still didn't know what they would find when they got there.

The path broadened slightly as they came towards Lady Naomi's clearing. They saw that the holo-projected boulder that usually hid Lady Naomi's workstation was switched off, and all her equipment was lit up. That familiar sweet perfume filled the air, and there was Mallan: standing with his back to them, looking up at the huge holo-screen as he played with her scanners.

"Ugh," breathed Charlie. "Sometimes I hate being right."

Amelia concentrated on the image Mallan was manipulating. It took a second to realize it wasn't Chloros or any other alien planet he was searching. He zoomed into the landscape, all rendered in the weird blues and greens of infrared, and Amelia recognized a distinctive curve with a protruding lump on one side.

It was Forgotten Bay and the gateway headland!

Mallan fiddled with the controls and the infrared was replaced by another filter. Perhaps it was the radiation scan Lady Naomi had used once, when they were looking for the starship in the sands of Egypt; now, like then, the whole screen went black. Mallan clicked his tongue and then the image zoomed in – or rather, three hot-pink spots zoomed out of the void.

Mallan hummed happily to himself and zoomed in again until the three pink spots were as large as they could be and still all fit on the screen at once. Then he brought up a night vision of the headland and overlaid it on the dots.

Amelia stifled a gasp. One dot – far bigger than the other two – was right over Tom's cottage. *The gateway*, she guessed. Hidden in the natural cave system under the headland, the mouth of the gateway opened directly under Tom's.

But the other two dots? One was very bright but a mere speck, and seemed to be right on the edge of the headland, where sheer cliffs dropped from a sickening height down to the surf below.

The other dot was larger but fainter, and seemed to be moving slightly. To Amelia's surprise, it was apparently on the other side of the clearing from them.

Mallan seemed surprised, too – his head snapped around to peer into the darkness and he began talking to himself.

"Well, well," he chuckled. "*Three* points. This is not at all what I was expecting. What a fascinating game this is turning out to be."

He left the workstation and sauntered into the shadows beyond it. Amelia strained her eyes, but of course, whatever energy was making the dot glow pink on the screen, it wasn't visibly glowing in real life. And of course, Mallan wasn't talking to himself.

"Tell me, sweet sister," he crooned. "Oh dear, long-lost heart of my heart – be a pet and tell me everything. Did you know about this all along?"

He re-emerged into the light of the workstation, his gorgeous face managing to look loving and sorrowful and stern all at the same time, as he trailed behind him a long silver thread.

Charlie sucked in a breath and Amelia went cold all over, watching Mallan gently drawing the thread, hand over hand, towards him. They'd seen something like this once before, and then Amelia had seen it dozens of times since in her nightmares.

Slowly, an enormous watery bubble drifted out of the shadows, bobbing obediently at the end of the thread. Inside, tears streaming down her face, was Lady Naomi.

A bubble doesn't prove anything, Amelia hoped desperately. *I bet lots of people have that weapon.*

"Oriana, darling," Mallan sighed. "This is so much more painful for me than you will ever know. I hate this, I really do, but if only you'd tell me the truth, none of this –" he waved an elegant hand at the bubble "– would be necessary."

He smiled that devastating smile, and this time Amelia knew exactly who it reminded her of. She felt like she was going to throw up.

"You obviously know more about all this than anyone guessed," he chided Lady Naomi. "So why don't you make it easy on yourself and tell me everything? From the beginning, sweetness: what's your connection with the component?"

Lady Naomi's eyes were closed, refusing to look at Mallan, but the tears kept flowing. Her narrow shoulders trembled as she sobbed silently, but her back was straight and her mouth was set.

"Oriana?"

She shook her head and then turned her back on him.

Mallan sighed heavily. "Right," he said. "Well, if you won't play nicely with me, then I don't need to keep playing either."

He reached up to his neck, slipped his finger into the flesh of his throat and pulled away a small cylinder. Switching off his holo-disguise, Mallan disappeared.

Standing in his place, stretching out the kinks from his long neck and unfurling his sinuous tail, was an alien even more beautiful than Mallan himself. The soft, matte-black skin of his salamander body absorbed the light from Lady Naomi's equipment so completely that he almost disappeared into the night. His wide, red eyes narrowed merrily.

"Now then, my darling," murmured Krskn. "No more games. I don't yet understand how you're involved in this, but I recognize a treasure when I see one. I rather think I'll be keeping you."

CHAPTER EIGHT

Krskn looked around at Lady Naomi's work-station. He was utterly calm, unhurried.

"Now, sweet sister," he said. "Is there anything here you'd like to take with us?"

Lady Naomi, her back still turned to him, said nothing. She lifted a hand and roughly wiped away her tears, lifted her chin and opened her eyes. Amelia saw a look of fierce resolve there, and then a flash of shock. She'd seen them! Perfectly able to see in the dark, Amelia and Charlie must have been embarrassingly obvious to her.

For a second, Lady Naomi's face brightened – the natural relief of knowing she wasn't quite as alone as she'd thought, Amelia guessed. But then she glared at them and looked pointedly towards the bush. She wanted them to get out of there.

"No," Krskn went on, chatting away as if he and Lady Naomi were having tea together. "Of course, you're right. Once you see what the Guild has to offer, you won't miss any of this. And I don't really want to dirty my hands with Control trash. In fact, I don't think I want anyone messing around with it. Too nasty to even think about, isn't it?"

He grinned broadly at Lady Naomi, and then shot a blast of laser fire into the central control panel. There was a flash of blue light as the entire system short-circuited, and the smell of burned plastic filled the clearing.

Charlie hissed something vicious in Greek, and Amelia couldn't agree more. They already knew Krskn was evil and cruel, but wrecking Lady Naomi's equipment was just spiteful.

But she was also furious with herself. With them all, actually.

She thought back to Mallan's arrival with sudden clarity. Just as Tom had been about to check him for a holo-emitter, he'd dropped Lady Naomi's name and thrown them all off track. How had they been so easily diverted? And how had James not guessed that the holo-projector could be programmed with fake images as easily as Earth animators could generate a cartoon? And how had she and Charlie not caught on to that poisonously charming smile?

It wasn't as if Grawk hadn't done his best – he'd noticed *something* and tried to let them know. But then that perfume Krskn was wearing had somehow thrown him off. Or made him so sick, he wouldn't come near Krskn again.

Charlie jabbed Amelia with his elbow. Krskn was shutting down the workstation, leaving them in deeper darkness, but before the last of the lights went out, Lady Naomi stared right at them both and mouthed something. *Go to Tom.*

Krskn left the clearing, Lady Naomi in the bubble drifting after him.

"Did you see that?" Charlie whispered as soon as they were alone.

"But Tom's not at his cottage, and Lady Naomi wouldn't know that."

"Yeah, but your dad is, and at least we'll be in the right place."

Amelia nodded. "You do that. I'm following Krskn."

"Are you nuts? You can't go after him alone."

Amelia was already getting to her feet. Whispering so urgently she was almost hissing, she said, "There's no time to argue – he's getting away. And I'm not going to *fight* him, but we have to know what he's doing and *someone* has to be with Lady Naomi, no matter what happens."

Charlie opened his mouth, his refusal all over his face, but Amelia cut him off. "I'm sorry," she said, "but this is my decision, and I'm not talking about it."

He frowned, angry at her, but said, "Fine. Just be careful."

She nodded, and set off in the direction Krskn had taken, already regretting her bravado. Not that she was turning back. She heard Charlie crunching back along the path they'd arrived on, and then his footsteps faded away and she was alone.

Alone, and following Krskn. *Insane*.

She closed her eyes for a second. There were no paths through the bush here, and she could see very little in the moonlight – not enough to pick up on the tiny snapped branches and scuffed rocks she needed to track Krskn, anyway. But she remembered that pink dot on the cliff's edge, and if she got her bearings right before she started ... she thought she could find him. And, more importantly, find Lady Naomi.

She moved as quickly as she dared, listening for Krskn, praying he couldn't hear her, and then heard something else entirely: the ocean. She was close now, and in more danger than ever.

The cliffs were nearly vertical, and their edges not only unstable but disguised by clumps of grass that grew out so thickly you couldn't tell where the ground gave way to sky. Amelia had to stay close enough to the edge to see where Krskn was going, yet not so close that she risked slipping.

She scrabbled over loose stones, grabbing hold of any skinny tree or crack in the rock she could, not trusting her feet for a minute.

The cliffs were so high here that the waves were a dull roar below them, but the noise gave some cover to her scuffling progress.

She slipped, twisting her ankle on a deceptive tree root, and a spray of tiny rocks clattered over a boulder and then vanished into the abyss.

Amelia gulped, moved more carefully still, and then saw Krskn himself slip out of the bush ahead of her. She froze as he strode to the very edge of the cliff, so close his toes must have been curling over the rim. The bubble with Lady Naomi was beside him. He'd been slower than she'd expected – probably hindered by the bubble, which must have gotten caught on every branch and twig along the way.

Without hesitation, Krskn dropped the slivery thread – the bubble stayed right where it was, as though anchored – and walked over the cliff's edge. Ridiculously flexible and strong, Krskn's salamander claws gripped the vertical face of the cliff as easily as they stood on flat ground. Amelia had seen him strolling down a carved column before, but that was nothing compared to seeing him wandering down the escarpment as though the height of it, the terrifying drop into the waves below, was nothing.

She crept closer to the edge of the cliff herself, horribly fascinated, disgusted but unable to look away as he sniffed the air and then headed for a crevice farther down.

With a guilty start, she remembered Lady Naomi, and hurried carefully to her bubble. She was only about six feet away when she saw Lady Naomi shaking her head, furious.

Amelia paused.

Go away, Lady Naomi mouthed. *Go now – go!*

But Amelia couldn't leave her. She crept forward again and stretched out a hand to grab the bubble's thread, and saw a flicker of movement out of the corner of her eye. Her heart pounded as she realized not only how close she'd gotten to the edge of the cliff, but that it was Krskn's tail that had caught her attention – he was coming *back*.

She looked at Lady Naomi, who had seen it too, and now covered her face with her hands, distraught.

"It's the canister," Amelia whispered. "That's where you hid it!"

Amelia leaned out, saw how far Krskn had gone, and felt dizzy. "That's where you hid it? But how –"

Then she hustled back from the edge of the cliff, terrified Krskn would see her, and – feeling guilty again – hid herself behind a rock. There wasn't enough time to rescue Lady Naomi. It was all she could do to keep out of Krskn's way herself.

She saw him walk back up and over the edge of the cliff, his eyes bright.

"Look, look!" he crowed to Lady Naomi, waving the canister at her. "Not a bad hiding place, I'll give you that. Obviously it was no problem for me, but then," he grinned and came close to the bubble, winding the silver thread through his fingers. It was a gesture that was strangely... affectionate? He chuckled. "Nothing's going to be a problem for me, ever again."

He began to walk back into the bush, still happily talking about himself to Lady Naomi.

"I can't begin to tell you what this means to me, pet. Debts cleared, scores settled, the right people thrilled to pieces with me, and all the wrong ones ruined forever. Ah, yes – with a victory of this magnitude, I wouldn't be surprised if the Guild Mistress names me as her successor."

Amelia followed at a distance as Krskn

wandered through a dense patch of bush, carefully guiding Lady Naomi's bubble under tangled branches. He was heading for a clump of large boulders at the top of a rise.

"Now this may seem a little rushed," he went on, "and I don't want you to feel you have to answer me straightaway, but I really sense a connection between us, don't you?"

Amelia blinked.

"I know," Krskn laughed, skipping lightly up the curve of the largest boulder. "It's mad and impulsive, but I can tell you feel it too. I really think I'm going to marry you, pet."

He hopped down from the boulder, and disappeared from Amelia's view. She paused, listening hard. She either gave up right now, or ... Or she followed.

After a second or two's more listening, she found another dirty tissue in her pocket, rubbed it against her armpit to pick up some sweat, and dropped it on the ground beside her. If Grawk ever came out of that drugged stupor Krskn put him in, maybe he'd find her trail. Hopefully, before it was too late to save her.

She braced herself, and then climbed after Krskn. It was much harder for her, and her sneakers slipped on the rocks several times, but at last she made it to the top of the boulder and saw where Krskn had gone. In the center of the clump of boulders was a gap in the rocks: the entrance to a tunnel. There were so many caves through the headland, they had to come out somewhere, but this was the first time Amelia had seen one.

She peered down – it looked as though it dropped for nearly six feet before the floor of the tunnel. If she went in, she wouldn't be able to get out again this way.

She jumped.

After a heavy landing on her twisted ankle, she began groping her way through the darkness – one hand out to feel the way, the other to shield her forehead from bumps.

She heard Krskn ahead, still making merry plans for his wedding. Lady Naomi said nothing in return. Amelia followed the sound, and then noticed a faint glow appearing ahead. Those luminous lichens that grew deep in the gateway caves must have crept all the way up here.

But the gateway – Krskn can't take the canister through it. Surely he knows that?

It was getting bright enough to see quite well now, the lichens growing more thickly the farther she went, with delicate blue and yellow fronds feathering out from the rock face. The tunnel twisted, and Amelia paused to listen before she turned the corner.

Nothing. Krskn must be going faster the more he could see. He could be quite a long way ahead already. She took a breath and came around the bend.

And there was Krskn, pointing a slender black tube directly at her face.

"Nosy little brat, aren't you?" he smiled. "I'd hoped you'd take the hint back at the clearing and go home with that dreadful boy, but here you are – still doggedly trailing after me. It's quite sweet really, isn't it?" He gloated at Lady Naomi, still trapped in the bubble. "She's got a crush on me. Not that you need to get jealous, my darling."

Lady Naomi shuddered, but Krskn didn't notice. His attention was fixed on Amelia.

She had no plan. Not a single idea came to her. Instead, she just stood frozen as Krskn shot a blast of white gel from the tube. It knocked her backward, but she never hit the ground.

She landed on the soft, unbreakable skin of a plasma bubble – *inside it*.

"I'll tell you what," said Krskn, picking up the bubble's silvery thread and dragging it along as he went to collect Lady Naomi's. "We'll let you be bridesmaid."

CHAPTER NINE

"This is just like old times," said Krskn, pulling the two bubbles behind him. He was bustling down the tunnels now that they were widening out. In fact, they were more like long chambers. They must be very close to the huge chamber of underground guest rooms that sat at the mouth of the gateway itself.

"No Keeper to save you this time, though," Krskn chortled. "No grawk to sniff me out. I'm sorry to leave him behind, though. What a beauty he's become since I saw you all last. I'd love to take him home with me; he'd make such a dramatic guard dog. Of course ..." He sounded thoughtful. "I do travel far too much to look after a pet. Not fair on the animal, is it? Never mind. He'd make a glorious fur rug instead."

Amelia wished she could be as self-controlled as Lady Naomi and ignore Krskn completely, but he made her so angry.

"You're disgusting!" she spat.

"Oh, that means so much, coming from you," he sneered. "We'll see how mouthy you are after you've been through the gateway, shall we?"

Amelia felt the blood drain from her. "Through the gateway? But you can't – don't you know what the canister will do? It will kill us all!"

"Is that what the Keeper told you? Your precious 'Leaf Man'? He's as ignorant and unimaginative as the rest of you. Don't you know what's in this canister?"

Lady Naomi, for the first time, stared at Krskn, listening.

"No," said Amelia, trying to sound braver than she felt. "Do you?"

"No, I don't," said Krskn, "but unlike you, I'm prepared to find out."

He fiddled with the top of the canister, then with a little "Aha!" of satisfaction, rotated a gear. A lid sprang open. Nothing happened that Amelia could see, and Krskn shook the canister, frowning.

"That's odd," he murmured. "What do you think, my love?" He looked up at Lady Naomi and then his mouth dropped open in astonishment.

Amelia turned and saw that Lady Naomi was beaming – a wild, delighted expression on her face, as though she were staring into the heart of all that was good in the world. Her face still glistened with tears, but now she was almost radiant. She fixed her eyes on Krskn and raised a hand.

Amelia thought she was going to wave or maybe threaten him with a fist or something, but that seemed very unlike Lady Naomi. Amelia pressed both hands against the skin of her own bubble, but knew that it was useless. Soft and wobbly and thinner than a rubber swimming cap, the bubbles were so strong they might as well have been made of bulletproof glass.

But Lady Naomi seemed to have forgotten this. Almost carelessly, as lightly as sweeping aside the bead curtains on the door at Archie's grocery, she brushed her hand through the membrane of her bubble and stepped lightly to the ground. The ruptured skin collapsed behind her.

"Impossible!" Krskn backed away, clutching the canister tightly, his eyes wide, but Amelia could see he was fascinated.

"Magnificent!" he murmured, and then Lady Naomi sprang at him, landing only six feet away.

There was no physical change in Lady Naomi that Amelia could see – she wasn't taller or musclier, she hadn't turned green or grown wings – and yet you could tell she was brimming over with power. Krskn must have felt it too because he pulled a new weapon from his belt and pointed it squarely at Lady Naomi.

"Come now, my darling," he crooned. "I don't want to kill you. Really."

Lady Naomi didn't flinch. She walked towards Krskn almost eagerly, as though his weapon were nothing more than a toy. And then he shot –

It was too quick for Amelia to even blink, but she saw Lady Naomi flick her hand sharply and the bolt of laser fire was swatted back at Krskn. It struck the rock just an inch to one side of his head, and he was so shocked that he just stood there, frozen, as Lady Naomi plucked the gun from his hand.

Then he snapped back to himself, and before Lady Naomi could snatch away the canister too, he darted away and slithered into a crevice in the cavern's wall. In the silence that followed, there was a delicate mechanical noise, and Amelia guessed he'd closed the canister.

Lady Naomi, the weapon still pointed in Krskn's direction, came back to Amelia, and with the same casual gesture, tore through her bubble. Amelia hopped out of it before it could deflate on top of her, and landed awkwardly on her bad ankle. A pain shot up her leg, but she barely noticed because Lady Naomi had staggered sideways, one hand to her chest.

"Are you OK?" Amelia said, limping to her side. "What happened?"

"I don't know." Lady Naomi sounded dazed.

Her eyes were slightly unfocused, but Krskn's gun was still in her hand and she kept it pointed towards the crevice.

Amelia guessed Lady Naomi's loss of strength had something to do with the canister, but there was no time to puzzle it out now. From this angle, Amelia could see straight into Krskn's crevice.

Krskn was no longer there.

"My dearest treasure," he purred, and Amelia cringed to realize he was clinging to the roof of the cavern above them. Far from being fazed by the laser gun pointed at him, he seemed genuinely pleased to be near Lady Naomi. "You just become more deliciously intriguing every moment we're together. Tell me, my love, and be honest with me at last: what *are* you?"

Lady Naomi gathered herself, and it seemed to Amelia that though the loss of power had unbalanced her for an instant, it hadn't done her any harm. And even without the canister's super-boost, Lady Naomi was still remarkable. Plus she was furious with Krskn.

She narrowed her eyes and took aim at his chest, but Amelia heard footsteps echoing down stone steps – the steps that led down from Tom's cottage to the other side of the gateway's mouth. She must be wrong: this cavern couldn't lead to the underground guest rooms – the footsteps were too near for that. This must be a *third* approach to the gateway. Tom had told her how complicated the caves were, but now she despaired.

"Goodness, this is getting busy," said Krskn lazily. His tail twitched, but otherwise he was little more than a shadow on the cave's roof.

Lady Naomi hesitated, distracted by this unexpected complication. That split second was the chance Krskn needed. He darted forward, right over Lady Naomi's head, and swiped at her with his tail. In the tiny moment it took for her to leap aside and take aim again, Krskn had already crossed the cavern roof.

Being a natural cave, there were no straight lines or angles. The roof gradually curved around and sloped into the wall, so that Krskn was now above Amelia, and also slightly behind her. He was so close, she could smell that sweet perfume still lingering on him.

And then Dad (holding Tom's shotgun) and Charlie jogged into the cavern's far end.

"Be careful!" Amelia shouted. "It's Krskn. And he's got the canister!"

Krskn tutted, "So rude, and me almost family now."

Turning her head a fraction, Amelia saw he had crept lower still so that he was now completely shielded behind her. Unless Dad or Lady Naomi were counting on her to jump out of the way faster than Krskn could follow, the two guns were effectively useless.

Dad turned the shotgun away, not willing to point it anywhere near Amelia, while Lady Naomi tried to inch her way to a better firing position off to one side. Amelia considered bolting for Dad, leaving Krskn to Lady Naomi, but before she could move, the ground vibrated under her feet and a nasty, acrid air wafted through the cavern. A wormhole had connected with the gateway.

"Perfect timing!" said Krskn. "It's almost ... almost as if I'd *planned* this whole caper right down to the last detail."

"You can't take the canister with you," Dad called. "You'll – well, never mind about probably turning Earth inside out and sucking the whole solar system into the Nowhere – you'll kill *yourself* if you do this."

Krskn laughed. "I think you're right, but

wouldn't it be fun to try it and know for sure?"

"We're not going to stop you, Krskn," Dad went on. "We don't care where you go, just leave the canister. We won't even tell Control you were here."

"Hmm," Krskn mused. "That sounds ... sensible. I'm rather tempted, and really touched by your concern for me, Scott. Of course, I don't doubt your honesty for a second. I'm sure you really *would* let me leave."

Charlie looked at Amelia, hopeful.

"On the other hand," Krskn said, "I have to consider what I came for."

"What did you come for?" asked Dad. "Let's see if we can't help each other."

"Wonderful! You see, Amelia? That's real family teamwork. And manners."

Amelia ignored his purring voice and didn't look behind her again. She kept her eyes on Dad and Charlie, but she felt Krskn's warm, sweet breath on the back of her neck.

"Well," Krskn called. "I came for total control of the gateway and all the people and power and technology attached to it. Now, your turn, Scott: what do you want?"

"I was just hoping we could all live through this," said Dad. "Especially my daughter, if you don't mind."

"Hmm ..."

Amelia felt her hair shift under his breath.

"Ah, let me think this through ... No. Sorry, Scott. Power, riches, and infinite danger win out over mere life every time."

With a sudden jerk, he wrapped his arm around Amelia's waist and pulled her tight against him. Holding the canister to the side of her head like a weapon, he laughed, and sprinted back along the roof, over the heads of everyone and heading directly for the gateway.

"Stop!" bellowed Charlie. "You can't!"

But by the time the sound reached Amelia, it was too late – he already had. With a shriek of triumph, Krskn leapt from the roof of the cave into the open mouth of the gateway, canister in one hand, Amelia held firmly with the other.

CHAPTER TEN

Amelia looked down and saw a shimmering circle – something like the wobble in the air you see above the road on a really hot day. But this shimmering was stronger, more solid, as though the shimmering were the real thing and the rest of Earth were the mirage.

And then, faster than blinking, they had fallen into it, through it, and Amelia, still hugged tightly against Krskn's wiry body, was through the gateway and inside a wormhole.

Once, when she was six years old, Amelia had been in a car accident. Not a bad one, just a minor fender bender at the traffic lights, but she'd never forgotten how time seemed to stop as she watched the other car veering into them. The crash was over in less than a second, but while it was happening, it seemed like minutes had passed.

In the same way, though it probably lasted less than a minute, Amelia felt herself falling forever, being sucked along the wormhole. She saw smooth, almost fluid walls around her, in a color she couldn't comprehend, and knew somehow that she was inside another ... she didn't know exactly what. There was nothing on Earth like this. But Amelia knew one thing instinctively: the gateway was more than just physics. It was *alive*.

And then, the canister beside Amelia's head

began to radiate heat, burning her ear, and still they rushed deeper into the wormhole – not so much falling as being pulled, and accelerating as they went. Krskn clutched Amelia more tightly, and she was so frightened she was actually glad to have his arms around her. Right at that moment, even her worst enemy was better than being alone.

And yet, it was somehow beautiful too – she'd never imagined that terror and wonder could exist together so completely. She was convinced that she was about to die, and yet what a marvelous death it would be – speeding through impossible space, feeling surrounded by a life that was so much older and bigger and greater than hers in every way ...

The canister burned hotter again, and she felt her ear begin to blister, but it was nothing to her now. Krskn's smell had been swept away, and instead something stronger, purer was engulfing them. Amelia would forever remember it as the smell of diamonds, but now she just tried to breathe it in as deeply as she could.

Then suddenly a wave of energy rushed down on them in the other direction – a wall of heat that was invisible but might as well have been solid. Amelia's heart swelled with even greater fear and delight as she and Krskn were tumbled over and over, and then buffeted back the way they had come. She collapsed at the foot of Tom's stairs, panting on the floor of the cavern, her ankle throbbing, the side of her face roaring with the burns.

The gateway had *spewed them out*.

Krskn was no longer with her, but she didn't think of that. She huddled against the sandstone steps, shivering, nauseous, relieved and unspeakably disappointed, as a cloud of *things* shrieked and battered their way past her.

The gateway heaved and groaned again, and another blast of hot air gusted through the caves, this one so violent that the luminous lichen was stripped off the walls, leaving dark, blank patches behind.

Amelia cringed into the cave floor, all the wonder gone now; now she was just scared of being pulverized by the wind against the rock walls. Krskn, Lady Naomi, her dad and Charlie must have been caught up in it too, perhaps only an arm's length away, but with all the noise and fury, her eyes shut tight against the stinging sand whipping past her, she might as well have been the only person alive.

Then everything fell quiet, the wind died to a faint sigh, and Amelia realized she was alive. Alive and home. Better yet, she heard a groan that could have only been Charlie, and then Dad calling hoarsely, "Amelia!"

She was filthy with dirt, every inch of her body encrusted with it, even the insides of her nostrils, and she ached all over. As well as her ear and ankle, her knees and ribs were battered too – she must have hit the floor hard when the wormhole expelled her.

But it was over. The gateway had closed again.

Amelia was still trying to decide if she could stand up yet, or whether she'd lie for just a bit longer, when Charlie sat down next to her. He was wheezing, spitting out bits of lichen, and his hair was full of dust, but he was smiling.

"You're OK!"

"Am I?" Amelia asked. "I wasn't sure yet."

"Well, you're here," Charlie amended. "And you're alive, and I'm so glad to see you."

Amelia sighed, and decided to try to sit up. Everything hurt, but nothing seemed broken, and she'd probably be fine once she rinsed out her mouth and got an icepack on her ear.

She almost forgot there was anything else to worry about when she heard Lady Naomi shout, "I see you!"

She and Charlie both jumped, and turned to see Krskn creeping out on all fours from behind a cave wall. He was a shabby sight, his red eyes the only Krskn-like thing left of him. His black salamander skin was now a dull, dusty brown, and he looked shrunken and pathetic, recoiling from Lady Naomi.

He croaked, "Wait! I –"

But Lady Naomi didn't give him a chance to finish. She shot him with one of his own weapons, and he crumpled to the floor without another sound.

Dad and Lady Naomi locked Krskn into one of the sealed glass guest rooms of the underground cavern just through the next bend in the tunnel. Amelia and Charlie, for once, didn't try to help. They were both happy to sit quietly and enjoy being safe and still.

Then Dad ruined everything by asking, "Did anyone see where the canister ended up?"

He and Lady Naomi began searching the caves, and after ten minutes or so with no success, Amelia and Charlie wearily got to their feet and joined in.

"Well, I don't know," said Dad, scratching his head. "Given how strong that wind was from the gateway, it could have blown a long way into the tunnels. And into any one of the tunnels. We could be searching for hours."

Lady Naomi made a disgusted noise. "And I can't even scan for it."

Dad was surprised. "Why not?"

"Krskn destroyed my workstation."

"Oh, Naomi." Dad groaned with real distress. "I'm so sorry. What a low blow ..."

Lady Naomi shrugged and looked away. "Oh, well, it's done now. But it means we'll have to keep searching manually."

"At least until we can get Control here," Dad started, then corrected himself. "Or I suppose we'll have to check with Tom and the Keeper whether we can tell Control about the canister, even now." He sighed. "Right, well, let's at least go and get James to help us map out the area, and then –"

Without warning, Amelia threw up, and began shivering violently.

"Oh, cookie!" cried Dad, hurrying over and putting his arms around her even as she tried to spit out the foul taste of sick. As if she wasn't feeling gross enough already.

Dad wiped her face with the edge of his T-shirt, and then picked her up like she was still a little kid. "Sorry, Lady Naomi. I'm going to have to leave you alone until I send James down."

Amelia, utterly exhausted, snuggled into Dad's neck as he began to trudge back the long tunnel to the hotel library's hidden trapdoor. She closed her eyes and listened to his footsteps.

"You too, Charlie," Dad called back. "You've had enough for one night."

Charlie didn't even argue.

The tunnel dimmed as they left behind the lichen caves, and eventually became so dark it didn't matter if Amelia opened her eyes or not. Dad and Charlie had to slow down and feel their way up the rough stone steps. It meant they were nearly home, though, and Amelia began to daydream about how good it would feel to be in her own bed.

And then she heard a strange noise. The closer they got to the hotel, the louder the ruckus: a mixture of human voices and an unrecognizable squealing.

Dad groaned. "Ah, don't tell me ..."

"The trapdoor's not open, is it?" asked Charlie.

"From the sound of it, yes. I just hope nobody's noticed it yet."

"I thought it was still night."

"It is."

"So then who –"

"Let's just wait and see," Dad interrupted him.

They plodded on faster, Amelia struggling a bit in Dad's arms. "I can walk," she murmured, but it wasn't very convincing.

"Shh." Dad tightened his hold and kissed the top of her head. "We're nearly there."

Amelia stayed still, too tired to insist, but she couldn't stop her mind from chattering on:

What if a human guest saw the tunnel? What if they heard the gateway? What if ...?

But her guesses were nowhere near bad enough. What they found as they emerged into the hotel was far worse than anything Amelia had been worrying about.

For a start, the trapdoor wasn't just open – it had been blasted off its hinges. The blowback from the gateway had exploded through it with such force, the splintered door was lying against the opposite wall. It must have sounded like a bomb going off.

Worse still, the tornado-strength wind had carried with it not just sand, but clods of luminous lichen and, bizarrely, hundreds – if not thousands – of tiny, enraged bats.

Amelia vaguely recalled something high-pitched flying over her head back there in the caves, but hadn't wondered what it could be.

Even if she had, she doubted she would have guessed yellow micro-bats. In a stupor of fatigue, she watched one crawling up the curtains. It was not much bigger than a fat huntsman spider, with a long purple horn on its forehead and double dragon's tails waggling behind it.

Alien, she thought dully.

And then she became aware of the screaming. A lot of screaming. Dad led Charlie out from the library into the lobby.

Every single guest must have been there, all in their pajamas. (Miraculously, all the aliens had still remembered to switch on their holo-emitters.) Human and alien alike, they were running amok. Mum and James were there, standing on the reception desk, trying to call out for calm, but it was far too late for that.

Lichen was hanging off the chandelier and picture frames, covering the floor, and giving the lobby a weirdly festive look. The air was hazy with cave dust, but above all of that, of course, were the bats. Screeching, dive-bombing, attacking the guests with their sharp horns, swooping in flocks, and spattering people with rancid droppings. It was the most disgusting, chaotic and ridiculous thing Amelia had ever seen.

Mum spotted them from her desk and jumped down, pushing her way through the panicking guests, and sweeping Dad, Amelia and Charlie up into one huge hug. She kissed the tops of their dirty heads, and then looked up at Dad.

"Where's Lady Naomi?" she asked.

"She's safe," said Dad, "but angry at herself, and embarrassed for having been taken for a fool."

"But none of us –" Mum began.

"It was Krskn," said Dad wearily. "So no, no one will blame her for falling for his act. But she's still blaming herself."

Mum sighed. "That poor, poor girl. Is that why she hasn't come back with you?"

Dad laughed bitterly. "No, that's the other thing: the canister's missing."

"OK." Mum squared her shoulders. "I should have guessed something dreadful had happened." She gestured at the roaring panic-stricken madness behind her. "But you're all fine, aren't you?"

She peered more closely at Amelia. "No, not really fine at all. What's happened to you, my little chicken?"

"Ah." Dad cleared his throat. "Krskn took her hostage and pulled her into a wormhole, and then it sort of exploded on them, and –"

Mum gasped in horror, and Amelia groaned and looked at Charlie. She expected one of his knowing looks in return, but instead saw, well, not curiosity. And not sympathy. Was it … jealousy?

"We'll talk about it later," said Dad. "Right now, though, these kids need some sleep."

The next morning, all the human guests wanted to check out before breakfast, and Mum and Mary had a hard time convincing them to stay until "compensation" could be arranged. What they really meant was, no earthling could leave the headland until Control had come and had their say.

Amelia and Charlie wondered what that say would be. Of the top three Control agents on Earth, Ms. Rosby was quite happy for humanity to learn about aliens. Arxish, on the other hand, was definitely not. As for Stern ... they'd never met him yet, though they'd seen the back of his head as he got out of Mr. Snavely's car with the others and poor Tom, whom they'd given a ride home. The four of them were down at Tom's now.

Somehow, though, Amelia and Charlie couldn't get too upset about any of it. It was just too good to sit in the early sunshine, Amelia digging her hands into the lawn as if to prove to herself she really was firmly on Earth, and against all odds, they'd not only lived through another attack from Krskn – they'd actually captured him.

And Lady Naomi was staying (though Amelia was too tactful to tell Lady Naomi how glad she was about that – not just yet, anyway). Grawk had completely recovered from the tranquilizer dart, and was now sitting guard outside Krskn's tank.

"If only someone would bring us food, everything would be perfect," sighed Charlie.

"Will brownies do?" Lady Naomi sat down beside them and set a plate on the grass.

Charlie crammed most of one in his mouth and moaned in contentment.

"How's it going down there?" asked Amelia. Last night felt like a million years ago – until she moved, that is. Then she felt every bruise and sprain and burn all over again.

Lady Naomi wrinkled her nose. "Lots of talking. Arxish is arguing for the hotel to be closed to human guests, and it sounds as though Ms. Rosby won't fight him on it."

"And us?"

"You're OK. Your dad's keeping his job, so you'll all stay here. None of that will change."

"Phew!" Amelia let go of the last bit of tension. "And how about Tom?"

Lady Naomi blushed and looked away.

"What's happened to him?"

"You mean apart from me turning my back on him after he raised me my whole life? Me telling him he wasn't a good enough reason to stay here just because my so-called *brother* –" She spat out the last word with such contempt she couldn't finish her sentence.

"I'm sure Tom will understand," said Amelia.

Lady Naomi snorted. "He does! That's the worst bit: I've been so thoughtless and selfish and ungrateful, and I'm so sorry I'd do anything to make it up, but Tom's still only worried about *me*. Like I'm the one who's been hard done by."

"Well, you sort of are," said Charlie, chomping into yet another brownie. "I mean, it's not like *Tom's* engaged to Krskn now."

Amelia rolled her eyes, but now that the dreaded name had come up, she had to ask. "And Krskn? What's happening with him?"

For the first time, Lady Naomi gave a real smile. "You've earned some serious respect from Control there. Even Arxish can't hide his happiness – it's going to look great on his resume that he was one of the three directors that brought in Krskn."

"*What?*" spluttered Charlie. "He did nothing!"

"No, no – he was in charge when good things happened, so he'll get the credit for it. That's how these things work."

"That sucks!"

Lady Naomi shrugged. "What concerns me is how Krskn is taking it all. He had Control all around him, staring and pointing and cracking jokes at his expense, and he just yawned."

"He slept through his arrest?" Amelia asked. "Maybe the drugs from that dart were still working."

"Oh, no, he was wide-awake." Lady Naomi shuddered. "He wasn't sedated, he was *bored*."

"Yeah, well." Charlie took another brownie. "That's Krskn, I suppose. He's evil and crazy, but you've got to admit: he's cool."

"Charlie!" Amelia shoved him.

"Well, he is! I don't mean I think he's awesome, but he does have style. And nothing much bothers him, does it?"

"Hmm." Lady Naomi stared out over the headland. She looked completely bothered by Krskn.

Charlie, oblivious, went on, "And he *loves* you, Lady Naomi, so you've got to give him points for that. He has good taste."

Lady Naomi made a disgusted face. "Cheers, Charlie. That makes me feel much better."

"Does that mean you're not going to marry him, then?"

Lady Naomi snorted. She and Amelia gave him a hard shove each, one on each side so that he was squished between them. He squeaked in outrage.

"No, thanks, Charlie," said Lady Naomi, smiling and passing him another brownie. "Right now, I feel pretty lucky to stay right here with all of you. You're enough family for me, I think."

SEVEN GREAT ADVENTURES

Cerberus Jones

Cerberus Jones is the three-headed writing team made up of Chris Morphew, Rowan McAuley and David Harding.

Chris Morphew is *The Gateway's* story architect. Chris's experience writing adventures for *Zac Power* and heart-stopping twists for *The Phoenix Files* makes him the perfect man for the job!

Rowan McAuley is the team's chief writer. Before joining Cerberus Jones, Rowan wrote some of the most memorable stories and characters in the best-selling *Go Girl!* series.

David Harding's job is editing and continuity. He is also the man behind *Robert Irwin's Dinosaur Hunter* series, as well as several *RSPCA Animal Tales* titles.